DR. DRABBLE'S
REMARKABLE UNDERWATER
BREATHING PILLS

Written by
Sigmund Brouwer and Wayne Davidson
Illustrated by
Bill Bell

A DIVISION OF SCRIPTURE PRESS PUBLICATIONS INC.
USA CANADA ENGLAND

With love,
to Karen, Courtney,
and Chelsea

vw
91-206208
ISBN: 0-89693-903-0

VICTOR BOOKS
A division of SP Publications, Inc.
Wheaton, Illinois 60187

Dr. Drabble was a genius inventor. He traveled around the world with PJ and Chelsea's parents, who were missionaries. The All-in-One Traveling Apparatus was floating near Australia in the shallow waters of the reefs.

Chelsea carried a tray of cookies to her brother PJ on the deck of Dr. Drabble's All-in-One Traveling Apparatus.

"I'm sure I *won't* like this batch," PJ told her. "The first three batches were terrible."

"But I added double the amount of chocolate chips," she protested.

PJ looked carefully at the cookies. "How can you see the chocolate chips? These are burned really dark."

Chelsea scowled. "Just scrape them. Dr. Drabble does it to his toast."

PJ wanted a reason not to eat those cookies. But he didn't want to hurt his sister's feelings. He shouted for their pet skunk. "Wesley! Wesssleeey!"

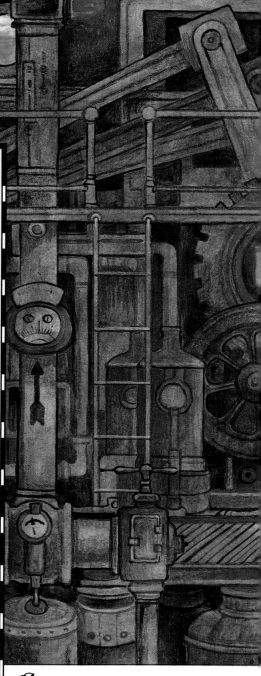

PJ became very proud of himself at that moment. Since he happened to know that Wesley was snugly asleep under a bench in Dr. Drabble's laboratory, he could now fool Chelsea.

"Wesley may be in great danger," he said. "We must search for him."

"What!?!" Chelsea nearly shouted. She forgot all about her cookies.

PJ nearly smiled. His plan had worked. It was too bad for him that he forgot friends shouldn't lie to each other.

"Yes," PJ said as his lie grew bigger. "I just remembered that Arnie Clodbuckle might have left him in the engine room while he was adjusting the controls this morning."

Arnie Clodbuckle was Dr. Drabble's assistant.

Chelsea believed her brother's lie, and soon both of them were in the engine room.

Chelsea searched everywhere. Then PJ snapped his fingers.

"Hey!" he blurted. "Maybe Arnie took Wesley to the laboratory."

It was the place where Dr. Drabble constructed his genius inventions.

As soon as they got there, PJ said, "Chelsea, why don't you look at that side of the room. I'll check this end."

While Chelsea was busy, PJ moved to the bench and grabbed Wesley.

"I found him!" PJ shouted.

Chelsea hugged her brother. "Let me reward you with my cookies."

PJ followed his sister back to the deck of the Brilliant All-in-One Traveling Apparatus. His lie had not saved him. He would have to eat one of the terrible cookies or his sister's feelings would be hurt.

He was saved by shouting farther down the deck.

"No! No!" someone screamed. "I can't swim!"

921965

It was Arnie Clodbuckle.

At the far end of the ship, Dr. Drabble was trying to push him over the rail into the ocean.

"You must go," Dr. Drabble said as he tried lifting one of Arnie's legs. "Assistants always volunteer for experiments."

"But I can't swim," Arnie wailed.

Chelsea interrupted. "What is Arnie testing now?"

"My Remarkable Underwater Breathing and Swimming Pills."

"Neat!" Chelsea grinned. "We'll try them for you!"

Dr. Drabble said, "You have to promise to stay close to the ship." He gave each of them a scuba mask, flippers, and one Remarkable Underwater Breathing and Swimming Pill.

"Oh," Dr. Drabble remembered. "The pills also let you talk with fish."

PJ, Chelsea, and Wesley got ready and then jumped into the water.

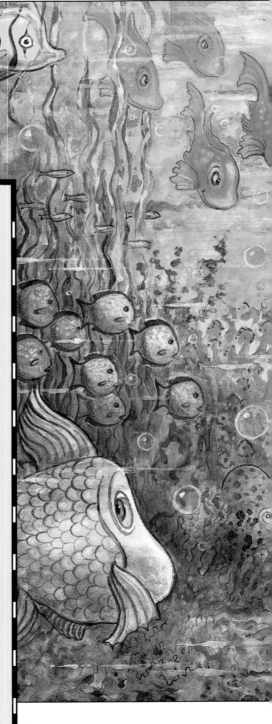

Soon they were swimming under the ship and having a great deal of fun.

The reefs around them were filled with all kinds and sizes of colorful fish.

"Look at that big, beautiful rainbow-colored fish!" Chelsea shouted happily.

A tiny minnow swam right up to her mask. "You don't have to shout," the minnow said crossly. "We're not deaf, you know."

Before Chelsea could apologize, the rainbow-colored fish bumped into her. "Watch where you're going," it said in a grouchy fish voice.

"Me? You're the one who needs glasses if you can't even see me."

The rainbow-colored fish stayed grumpy. "Glasses? What are glasses?"

Chelsea tried explaining, but it didn't work. Finally Chelsea turned to PJ. "Lend this fish your glasses. Then he'll know what I'm talking about."

"Just for a minute," PJ replied. "I need them back or I will be bumping into things." PJ carefully placed the glasses on the fish.

The fish jumped back. "Hey! You're not fish!"

It then looked at Wesley. "And that might be a fish but it sure is ugly."

Chelsea smiled. "I told you they worked, didn't I?"

PJ took his glasses back right away. He felt nervous without them.

Then the rainbow-colored fish smiled an evil fish smile. But since he was right — PJ and Chelsea weren't fish — they didn't recognize it as an evil smile.

"I want to be your friend," the fish lied. "My name is Murgatroyd."

PJ and Chelsea were too polite to tease him about his name.

"Would you like a pirate's treasure?" he continued. "It will make you very rich."

What PJ and Chelsea didn't realize was that Murgatroyd wanted to get them lost and steal PJ's glasses.

"Sure we would!" PJ and Chelsea said at the same time. They thought of all the toys they could buy. They even thought of how much money they could give to their mom and dad and Dr. Drabble and Arnie Clodbuckle as presents.

"Great," Murgatroyd said with a nasty smile. "It's just on the other side of the reefs."

"Hold it," PJ said. "The water is very deep on the other side of the reefs."

"Why does that matter?" Murgatroyd asked. "If you can breathe like a fish, you can go wherever fish go."

"That's right," Chelsea said quickly. "And think of how rich we will be."

PJ finally agreed.

On the other side of the reefs, the water was very deep and very dark.

PJ and Chelsea thought once again about the toys they could buy. So they followed Murgatroyd into the deep, deep water. Soon it was dark.

"It's hard to see," Chelsea said. "How will we find the treasure?"

Murgatroyd agreed. "It is dark. But if you lend me your glasses, I'm sure I'll be able to find it. I know it's close by."

PJ really wanted to find the treasure to buy some toys. This time, he gladly gave his glasses to Murgatroyd.

"Ha! Ha! Ha!" Murgatroyd laughed. "I've got what I wanted. Your glasses! I can see! I can see! And now you'll never see me again!"

Suddenly, Murgatroyd started swimming very fast.

"Wait!" PJ and Chelsea shouted as they tried to keep up. "We're lost."

Murgatroyd did not listen and soon he was gone. PJ and Chelsea stopped. They were alone.

"I think I see a shark," PJ moaned.

"I don't want to think about it," Chelsea trembled. "I just want to find the ship."

They tried starting back. But after a few minutes, it got even darker.

"Chelsea," PJ said in a small voice.

"Yes?"

"I think we're going in the wrong direction."

Chelsea nodded. "We're lost in the middle of the ocean!"

Before they could worry any longer, a small light appeared and grew larger as it came closer.

"Chelsea! PJ! Where are you?"

It was their dad. PJ and Chelsea swam toward him with relief. He had a diver's flashlight strapped to his head.

"Dr. Drabble forgot to tell you that the underwater pills only last an hour," Dad explained. "So they had me come looking for you."

When they reached the ship, Dad noticed PJ's glasses were missing. "Okay," Dad said. "I want to hear everything."

PJ and Chelsea told him about Murgatroyd and about the treasure and how they had dreamed about becoming rich enough to buy any toy they wanted.

"Well," Dad started. "As usual, you've learned things the hard way. I have two things to say about this."

He looked at them sternly. "One is that we should not be greedy. There are much more important things in life than money. Like *real* friends."

PJ remembered his lie and how he had fooled Chelsea into looking for Wesley. He decided he would never do that to a *real* friend again.

Then Dad grinned. "The second part is this. Now that Murgatroyd lied to you and has a new pair of glasses, it will be easy for him to spot this nice juicy worm."

Dad put the worm on a hook and cast it overboard. Sure enough, five minutes later, he caught that nasty fish named Murgatroyd. PJ was happy to get his glasses back.

And that night, everyone on the ship ate fish for supper.